The Ultimate Battle and Bible PROPHECY

THE ULTIMATE BATTLE AND BIBLE PROPHECY

WRITTEN BY
RICK OSBORNE
ED STRAUSS

ILLUSTRATED BY
JACK SNIDER

Zonderkidz

Zonder**kidz**.

The children's group of Zondervan
www.zonderkidz.com

The Ultimate Battle & Bible Prophecy
Copyright ® 2004 by Lightwave Publishing, Inc.

Requests for information should be addressed to:
Grand Rapids, Michigan 49530

ISBN: 0-310-70776-5

Library of Congress Cataloging-in-Publication Data

Osborne, Rick.
  The ultimate battle and Bible prophecy / Rick Osborne and Ed Strauss.
    p. cm.
  ISBN 0-310-70776-5 (pbk.)
  1. Eschatology--Juvenile literature. 2. Bible--Prophecies--Juvenile
literature. [1. Second Advent. 2. Bible--Prophecies.] I. Strauss, Ed,
1953- II. Title.
  BT886.3.O83 2004
  236'.9--dc22   2003025490

Zonderkidz is a trademark of Zondervan
Written by: Rick Osborne and Ed Strauss

Editor: Gwen Ellis
Art Direction and Interior Design: Michelle Lenger

Printed in United States of America
04 05 06 07/RRD/5 4 3 2 1

CONTENTS

THE TIME OF THE END!

If you know nothing about the Antichrist or the Great Tribulation, the Rapture or the Mark of the Beast, if you've never heard of the Battle of Armageddon, hey, it's probably 'cause you've been frozen inside an iceberg off the coast of Labrador for the last 2,000 years. While you're drinking hot chocolate and thawing out, you just *might* want to read the book you are holding in your hands. You have a lot of catching up to do.

Chances are, however, that you've already heard about the end-time, but you just can't figure it out. Last days? What's that? A week before summer holidays? Rapture? Is that Christian rap music? The Beast? Is he, like, some new wrestler? Patience … patience. All will be explained.

End-time Bible prophecy is an important subject because many Christians believe that we're living in the last days or that we're close to them. They believe that Jesus' second coming and the Great Tribulation will happen in our lifetime—in fact, practically tomorrow. Other Christians believe that Jesus' return is still a long way off.

If you've read a book on end-time prophecy, you might come away from it thinking that you now have things pretty much figured out. But there are *oodles* of books about the end-time, and they often interpret prophecy very differently from each other. That's because Christians have different opinions about what is going to happen and the order in which those things will happen.

Why so many different opinions? Well, a lot of end-time teaching comes from dreams and visions. In the books of Daniel and Revelation, where many Christians get their viewpoint of end-time events, we see visions and dreams of seven-headed dragons, fire-belching horses. Wild stuff! Sometimes the prophets wrote down what the visions meant, but a lot of times they just wrote down what they saw and didn't tell us what it meant. So people try to figure things out. You know, like a giant jigsaw puzzle.

End-time Bible prophecy really *is* a puzzle sometimes, but it's worth studying! The Bible says, "Blessed is the one who reads the words of this prophecy, and blessed are those who hear it and take to heart what is written in it" (Revelation 1:3).

We're not going to put all the pieces of the puzzle together for you. If we did that, we'd just be giving you *our* interpretation. Instead, we'll give you the puzzle pieces and show you how to think things through yourself. Prophecy is a mysterious and exciting topic and loads of fun to read about. One thing is for sure: after you've read this book you'll be glad you aren't frozen inside that iceberg off the coast of Labrador.

The *main* point of end-time Bible prophecy is that Jesus is coming back to earth and that we'll be spending eternity with him. It will be a wonderful world without pain or sorrow (Revelation 21:1–4). It is wonderful to look forward to what the Bible says, "No eye has seen, no ear has heard, no mind has conceived what God has prepared for those who love him" (1-Corinthians 2:9).

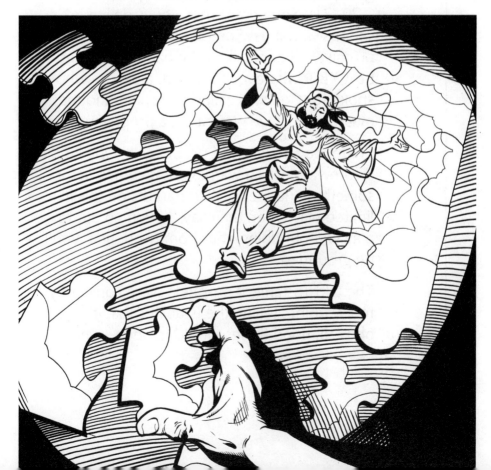

WHAT IS PROPHECY?

What does the word "prophecy" mean? Well, prophecy is when God's Holy Spirit spoke to men of God like Moses and Jeremiah and gave them a message for God's people (2-Peter 1:20–21). Sometimes these guys delivered serious warnings. Sometimes they gave happy promises. (People liked the happy promises best.) But whatever they said, a person who spoke for God was called a prophet and the message he gave was called a prophecy.

There are two kinds of prophecies. One kind is forewarning—a warning that comes before something happens. Your parents do this in a limited way when they say, "If you go out to play without doing your homework first, you'll be grounded."

The Old Testament prophets were constantly forewarning, telling the Israelites that if they obeyed, good things would happen—and

if they dis-
obeyed, bad
things would
happen (Isaiah
1:19–20).
This kind of
prophecy is
pretty simple.
Like Paul said, "A man reaps what he sows"
(Galatians 6:7).

The other kind of prophecy is foretelling.
Your parents *can't* do this, not even a little bit,
because they have no way of seeing forward
in time. But God is bigger than time and knows
everything. "Everything" includes everything
that's *been*, everything that is *now*, and everything that *will* be.

A good example of foretelling is when God
gave Daniel a vision about a goat with one horn
that defeated a two-horned ram. He said that
the goat was Greece and the horn was its first
great king who would conquer the ram, Media
and Persia (Daniel 8:1–8,19–22). Some 220
years after this prophecy, Alexander the Great,
king of Greece, *did* conquer Media and Persia!

HOW DOES PROPHECY COME?

Hebrews 1:1 says, "In the past God spoke to our forefathers through the prophets ... in various ways." What are some of the "various ways" that God spoke to and through the prophets? Well, sometimes they heard a voice (1-Samuel 3:1–14). Sometimes they heard a "gentle whisper" (1-Kings 19:12). Sometimes they only heard God's Spirit speaking in their mind and no one around them heard a thing. Sometimes angels appeared to people and gave them a message.

At times God showed people visions when their eyes were open, at other times when their eyes were closed, and sometimes even when they

were sleeping. Other times, men of God were caught up in visions. It was as if they were completely carried off to some other place (Ezekiel 8:1–3; Revelation 4:1–2).

Sometimes prophets spoke the message. Sometimes they wrote it (Habakkuk 2:2). Sometimes they drew pictures and acted out skits (Ezekiel 4:1–3). The prophet Isaiah even walked around naked for three years to get out a message (Isaiah 20:2–4).

But in whatever way God spoke through the prophets, it was the Holy Spirit giving the message. God's prophets didn't just make things up. "For prophecy never had its origin in the will of man, but men spoke from God as they were carried along by the Holy Spirit" (2-Peter 1:21).

WHAT IS PROPHECY FOR?

For those Christians who believe the end-time is yet to come, Daniel and Revelation along with parts of Isaiah, Matthew 24, 1 Corinthians 25, 1 and 2 Thessalonians show what will happen. What's the purpose of all this prophecy?

👁 *Prophecy gives us hope.* We may not know all the details about the future, but when we have an *idea* what it holds for us, things make better sense. We don't feel like we're lost in a giant corn maze. We know God has everything under control. We know he has a plan, and it's a good plan for us.

Prophecy shows us that things will turn out for the best in the end. God is in control of the world and eventually good will defeat evil. Knowing this can give us hope and comfort when we're going through hard times or persecution.

Prophecy warns us what to do. In the Bible, God warned his people and they got out of the way of danger. It's the same with last days prophecies: Those who believe the end-time is yet to come, believe that Christians will recognize prophecy as it unfolds. They will be able to avoid bad stuff.

Fulfilled prophecy shows the world that God is God. Only he can predict the future (Isaiah 46:9–10; Ezekiel 33:33). When the events predicted in the Bible happen, then many people will have faith in God.

FATALISTIC FREDDIE AND THE FANTASTIC FUTURE

Okay, so God knows what's going to happen in the future. Does that mean he has it all totally planned down to every tiny detail? Does that mean that at 3:03 P.M. on April 12, 2043, you will fall off a magno-ramp and bump your knee and there is absolutely *nothing* you can do to prevent that from happening? Is your future mapped out like a school play? No.

That kind of thinking is called fatalism. A fatalistic person says, "Why even try? No matter what I do, I can't change anything." Let's say that your teacher told you that you were in danger of failing math. If you listened to Fatalistic

Freddie you probably wouldn't study harder and turn in an extra assignment to bring your mark up. You'd just say, "Oh well, I was *meant* to fail math."

Sorry, that doesn't wash. It would be as if your parents asked you why your bedroom was messy and you said, "It was *meant* to be messy." That probably wouldn't go over very well. Now that we have that straight, go study for your math test and clean up your bedroom.

Yes, God has the big plan for humankind. The major events will happen, but *within* his big plan he allows us to choose how we will live our lives.

One of the main things that's going to happen, no matter what, is that Jesus is coming back. At some point, God is going to judge the world for the evil done. But remember, God's wrath isn't for Christians! The scary stuff is for the wicked, for those who rebel against God (1-Thessalonians 5:9; Revelation 9:4). Christians are going to miss out on the nasty stuff.

Fatalistic Freddie would be pleased to know that Jesus died so we could spend eternity ruling and reigning with him! And it will be such an awesome future that is full of so much good, exciting stuff that we'll "forget the former things" (Isaiah 43:18).

JESUS' FIRST COMING

We've been talking about prophecies of Jesus' second coming, but there were also prophecies about his *first* coming that came true 100 percent. The Old Testament talks about the coming Messiah (Savior—Jesus) several hundred times! Many prophecies were given long before Jesus was born. Some were given a thousand years before his birth! Here are a few of them.

DAVID IS HIS DADDY

The Jewish people believed that their Savior would be the son of King David of old. In fact, the title "Son of David" *meant* Savior! God had promised 560 years before Jesus was born that "I will raise up to David a righteous Branch, a

King who will reign wisely... In his days Judah will be saved" (Jeremiah 23:5-6). Well, Jesus was descended from David. When he went around Galilee and Judea, people often called him "Son of David" (Luke 20:41; Matthew 20:30-31).

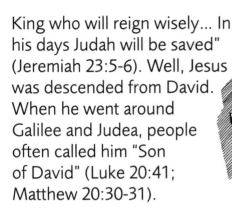

BIRTHPLACE PROPHESIED

King Herod asked the chief priests where the Savior would be born. They answered, "In Bethlehem ... for this is what the prophet has written: 'Bethlehem, in the land of Judah ... out of you will come a ruler who will be the shepherd of my people Israel'-" (Matthew 2:3–6; Micah 5:2). Micah prophesied this about seven hundred years before Jesus was born! And guess what—even though Mary and Joseph lived way up in Nazareth in the north of Israel, they ended up being forced by Rome to travel to Bethlehem just before Jesus was born. So Jesus *was* born in Bethlehem after all (Luke 2:1–7).

BORN OF A VIRGIN

Over seven hundred years before Jesus was born, Isaiah prophesied, "The virgin will be with

child and will give birth to a son" (Isaiah 7:14).
This is exactly what happened! Before Joseph
and Mary were married and Mary was a virgin,
"she was found to be with child through the
Holy Spirit" (Matthew 1:18–23).

THE SAVIOR BETRAYED

A thousand years before Jesus was born,
David prophesied that the Messiah would be
betrayed. Psalm 41:9 says, "Even my close
friend, whom I trusted, he who shared my
bread, has lifted up his heel against me." Jesus
said this prophecy was fulfilled in him—and it
was! Immediately after he shared bread with
Judas Iscariot, a close friend, Judas left the
house and betrayed Jesus (John 13:18–30;
18:2–3).

THIRTY SILVER COINS

The prophet Zechariah talked about a man who
was paid thirty pieces of silver and who then
said, "I took the thirty pieces of silver and threw
them into the house of the LORD to the potter"
(Zechariah 11:12–13). Guess what happened
550 years later! When Judas betrayed Jesus, the
priests paid him thirty silver coins. Later, Judas
tried to take the money back but the priests
said, "No way," so Judas chucked the coins on
the temple floor. The priests were down on
their hands and knees picking up coins. The

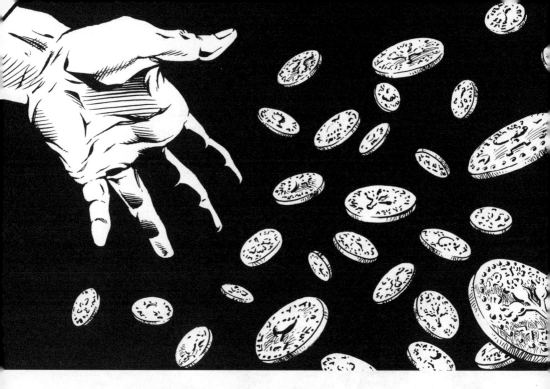

coins were blood money. So they used them to *buy a field from a potter* (Matthew 26:14–15; 27:3–8)!

THE CRUCIFIED SAVIOR

The Jewish people didn't dream that their Savior would be crucified, nailed by his hands and feet to a cross. Yet nearly a thousand years before this happened David prophesied about it in Psalm 22.

Verse 1 says, "My God, my God, why have you forsaken me?" These are the very same words Jesus cried out while dying on the cross (Matthew 27:46).

Verses 7–8 say, "All who see me mock me; they hurl insults, shaking their heads: 'He trusts in the LORD; let the LORD rescue him. Let him deliver him, since he delights in him.'-" This was *exactly* how Jesus' enemies mocked him (Matthew 27:39–43).

Verses 14–16 say, "I am poured out like water,

and all my bones are out of joint ... they have pierced my hands and my feet." These verses describe what it's like to be crucified, and all of this happened to Jesus!

Verse 18 says, "They divide my garments among them and cast lots for my clothing." These prophecies were fulfilled down to the last detail (John 19:23–24).

DIED FOR OUR SINS

Isaiah 53 is one of the most amazing chapters in the Bible! If you've never read it, make sure you do! Verses 3–6 describe how the Savior would be "pierced for our transgressions." Verse 6 says, "the LORD has laid on him the iniquity [sin] of us all." This is the message of salvation: we are all sinners but Jesus died to pay the price for our sins (John

10:11). Isaiah not only predicted what would happen 650 years before it happened, but also he told *why* it needed to happen.

BURIED WITH THE RICH

Isaiah 53:9 says, "He was assigned a grave with the wicked, and with the rich in his death." When Jesus was crucified he died between two wicked criminals. When Jesus was dead, he was buried in the grave of Joseph of Arimathea, a rich man (Matthew 27:37–44; 57–60).

RAISED FROM THE DEAD

Jesus prophesied several times that he would be killed *and* that he would later rise from the dead (Matthew 16:21; Luke 24:6–8). In Psalm 16:10, a thousand years before Jesus lived on earth, David prophesied, "You will not abandon me to the grave, nor will you let your Holy One see decay." Jesus died and was buried, but he stayed less than three days in the grave. Then God raised him back to life (Acts 2:25–31). His body had no time to decay.

ODDS OF FULFILLING ALL THE PROPHECIES

These are just a few of the many prophecies Jesus fulfilled. They prove that he is the Savior. Some critics argue that lots of people could have fulfilled these prophecies. *Not a chance!*

For example, the odds of someone fulfilling just eight of the main prophecies Jesus fulfilled are more than a *hundred thousand trillion to one*. That's one chance in 100,000,000,000,000,000. That's like dumping silver dollars over the entire state of Texas until it's covered two feet deep, then blindfolding someone and telling them he or she has only one chance to find the *one* coin with an "X" marked on it.

People are amazed that God knew hundreds or thousands of years ahead of time exactly what would happen. But hey, God knows *every* detail of the past and present. He knows what's coming, too! Nothing surprises him. It's no wonder that Jesus said we shouldn't worry (Matthew 6:34). He knows what will happen in your life if you trust and follow him. He also knows what will happen if you don't. Tell him that you love him and want his best for your life. Then trust that he's on the job as you follow him.

Reading and Taking It to Heart

Blessed for Reading

Some visions and prophecies are fun to read, *but* it's tough to figure out what in the world they mean. Just remember, Revelation 1:3 says, "Blessed is the one who reads the words of this prophecy, and blessed are those who hear it and take to heart what is written in it." It *doesn't* say, "Blessed is the one who reads and understands," because you won't always understand.

Even if you don't understand, keep reading. Give it thought. When Jesus talked to his disciples, they understood some of what he said. Later on they understood more. Jesus told the religious leaders, "Destroy this temple, and I

will raise it again in three days" (John 2:19–22). At the time everyone thought he meant the temple of stone (Matthew 27:40). But after Jesus was raised from the dead the disciples realized he had been talking about the temple of his *body* coming back to life.

Jesus' disciples listened and took his words to heart, but they didn't pull their hair out because they couldn't understand. When the event happened, God reminded them that it had been predicted (see John 12:16). Jesus promised, "the Holy Spirit ... will remind you of everything I have said to you" (John 14:26). So learn about prophecy. Then when it's fulfilled, the Spirit of God will reveal the meaning to you.

Seven Rules for Interpreting Prophecy

When your parents are driving on a dark back road in a heavy fog, they have to drive more carefully than they would on the freeway on a sunny day. They have to follow basic rules to keep your family safe: drive slowly, keep the lights on, keep the windows clean, keep their eyes open, and be ready to stop quickly. There are also basic rules to help you drive through the fog of prophecy.

👁 *Read and understand the simple stuff before tackling complicated stuff such as the book of Revelation.* As you study your Bible

and pray, you will gain understanding. The Holy Spirit has promised to help us understand God's Word. The important thing to remember is to live in a godly way. Ask the Holy Spirit to help you understand what you need to know about end-time events. Remember that even if you study a lot about end-time events, scholars have been studying for years and they don't all agree about what will happen or the order in which it will happen.

👁 *Focus on the stuff you can understand.* Again—we aren't meant to understand it all. Daniel once had such a mysterious vision that he gave up trying to figure it out. He just went back to work and didn't worry about it. He said, "it was beyond understanding" (Daniel 8:27). Another time, when the disciples asked Jesus a question about end-time prophecy, he told them, "It is not for you to know" (Acts 1:6–7).

👁 *There are many different end-time prophecy theories, and that's okay.* There's a series written by Tim LaHaye and Jerry Jenkins called Left Behind. These books are fun to read. But just remember that these novels are fiction, not fact. They describe events happening in a certain order, but that's only

one theory of how things will happen. No one can say for certain how all the end-time events will unfold.

👁 *Don't get caught up in little details.* Some people think the seven-headed dragon in Revelation 12:3 symbolizes China. Well, it might, or it might not. Some people theorize that a leader of Russia will be the Antichrist. Possibly, but who knows? It's okay to have interpretations, but no one *really* knows if a theory is right.

👁 *Don't just glom on to some prophecy theory and interpret every verse in the Bible by that theory.* That's a big temptation. It's like being *most* of the way through a complicated jigsaw puzzle and you want to say, "I worked on this thousand-piece puzzle, and I *finished* it." With Bible prophecy you *can't* neatly finish the puzzle. Nobody knows where all the details fit. So don't sweat it.

👁 *Don't be stubborn in your thinking.* A mind is like a parachute. It's no use to anyone unless it's open. Don't glue your mind to a certain theory or bolt your brain down to just one end-time interpretation. There's nothing wrong with saying, "This is how I see it," but be willing to listen to other people's points of view. Be open for God to teach you.

👁 *Let God interpret symbolic visions and dreams.* Joseph and Daniel, when asked what a dream meant, confessed that they couldn't figure it out. Only God could do that (Genesis 41:15–16; Daniel 2:26–28). When God gives a symbolic vision, he's the only one who can say what it means.

End-time prophecy can be lots of fun to study, but some people want to stuff and cram every single verse into one theory. Then they go around telling everyone else, "Yo, dudes! Good news! You don't have to think any more. I've figured it all out. You just need to accept my theory." Who would fall for a line like that? Hey, many of us often *do* swallow theories without thinking. We don't want to work hard studying, so we let someone else figure things out for us. Hold on! God wants us to read the Bible for ourselves and to think. He wants us to be like the Bereans, who "examined the Scriptures every day to see if what Paul said was true" (Acts 17:11).

DANIEL'S MOST AMAZING PROPHECY

Have you ever heard of Daniel's 70 "sevens" (also known as seventy weeks)? Daniel 9:24–27 is one of the most amazing prophecies in the entire Bible, and it's the foundation for a lot of end-time prophecy. So get out your pencil or your calculator, 'cause we're gonna do a bit of math.

Verse 24 gives the big picture. The angel Gabriel told Daniel, "Seventy 'sevens' are decreed for your people and your holy city to … seal up vision and prophecy …" Then Gabriel broke the 70 sevens into smaller chunks for

Daniel to wrap his brain around. Daniel 9:25–27
says:

> 👁 From the issuing of the decree to restore
> and rebuild Jerusalem until the Anointed
> One, the ruler, comes, there will be 7 "sev-
> ens," and 62 "sevens."

> 👁 After the 62 "sevens," the Anointed One
> will be cut off.

> 👁 The people of the ruler who will come will
> destroy the city and the sanctuary.

> 👁 He will confirm a covenant with many for
> 1 "seven."

> 👁 In the middle of the "seven" he will put an
> end to sacrifice and ... set up an abomination
> that causes desolation.

The Jewish people understood these "sevens"
were periods of seven years. So let's add up
the total number of years: 7 "sevens" (49 years)
plus 62 "sevens" (434 years) plus 1 "seven" (7
years) equals 70 "sevens" (490 years). Got that
so far?

Some years before Daniel received this vision,
the Babylonians had conquered Judah and
taken many Jews to Babylon—including Daniel.

Then the Babylonians destroyed Jerusalem and the temple. Now Daniel was prophesying that after a decree (royal command) was given to rebuild Jerusalem it would be rebuilt within 49 years, *and* then 434 years later the Messiah would come.

Guess what! In 457 B.C., a decree was issued

by King Artexerxes to rebuild Jerusalem. So do the math: 457 B.C. plus 483 years = A.D. 26. Jesus was born about 4 B.C., and when he was thirty (Luke 3:23), he was baptized and began his public ministry. This was in A.D. 26! Jesus showed up in Israel the very year that Daniel's prophecy said the Savior (the Anointed One) would come! Wow! Is that cool or *what!*

Of course, the Jewish people didn't understand the *next* part of Daniel's prophecy that said, "the Anointed One will be cut off." They thought the Messiah was going to sit on the throne of Israel and rule, *like*, *forever*. Instead, the Messiah was "cut off." This happened when Jesus was crucified.

And there's *more*! After the Messiah's death "the people of the ruler who will come will destroy the city and the sanctuary." Jesus was crucified in A.D. 30, and forty years later, in A.D. 70, the Romans destroyed Jerusalem and the sanctuary (the temple)! And think! God gave Daniel these predictions over 600 years before they happened.

What about the points that talk about the last seven years—the covenant and the abomination that causes desolation? Some Christians believe the last week happened during Jesus' lifetime and shortly after he died and rose again. Others believe they have not happened *yet* but will *soon*!

THE SECOND COMING

All Christians believe that Jesus will return to earth. That's basic and very important. But *when?* Jesus told his disciples, "No one knows about that day or hour" (Matthew 24:36). "Well, yeah, we don't know the day or hour, but we can know the year or the general times, right?" Not even. Jesus said, "It is not for you to know the times or dates the Father has set" (Acts 1:7). "Okay, okay, but at least we know he's going to return in our lifetime, right?" Nope. You can't even bank on that. Jesus said, "the Son of Man will come at an hour when you do not expect him" (Matthew 24:44).

The only thing we know for sure is that Jesus *will* return. Here are the main verses in the New Testament that teach us this.

"This same Jesus, who has been taken from you into heaven, will come back in the same way you have seen him go into heaven" (Acts 1:11).

"Immediately after the distress of those days the sun will be darkened, and the moon will not give its light; the stars will fall from the sky, and the heavenly bodies will be shaken. At that time the sign of the Son of Man will appear in the sky, and all the nations of the earth will mourn. They will see the Son of Man coming on the clouds of the sky, with power and great glory. And he will send his angels with a loud trumpet call, and they will gather his elect from the four winds, from one end of the heavens to the other" (Matthew 24:29–31). Mind you, some Christians believe that Matthew 24:29–31 is talking about the destruction of Jerusalem in A.D. 70

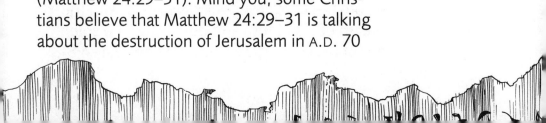

and that only the verses *after* verse 35 are talking about the Second Coming.)

"We will not all sleep [die], but we will all be changed—in a flash, in the twinkling of an eye, at the last trumpet. For the trumpet will sound, the dead will be raised imperishable, and we will be changed" (1-Corinthians 15:51–52).

"We who are still alive, who are left till the coming of the Lord, will certainly not precede those who have fallen asleep. For the Lord himself will come down from heaven, with a loud command, with the voice of the archangel and with the trumpet call of God, and the dead in Christ will rise first. After that, we who are still alive and are left will be caught up together with them in the clouds to meet the Lord in the air" (1-Thessalonians 4:15–17).

"Concerning the coming of our Lord Jesus Christ and our being gathered to him ... that day will not come until the rebellion occurs and the man of lawlessness is revealed, the man doomed to destruction. He will oppose and will exalt himself over everything that is called God or is worshiped, so that he sets himself up in God's temple, proclaiming himself to be God... And then the lawless one will be revealed, whom the Lord Jesus will overthrow with the breath of his mouth and destroy by the splendor of his coming" (2-Thessalonians 2:1–4,8).

"Look, he is coming with the clouds, and every eye will see him, even those who pierced him; and all the peoples of the earth will mourn because of him" (Revelation 1:7).

JESUS' PROPHECIES

When Jesus said that the temple would be destroyed, his disciples asked him, "When will this happen, and what will be the sign of your coming and of the end of the age?" (Whoa! Three questions in a row? Here come three answers in a row.) Jesus first described the signs of the end of the age, then the destruction of Jerusalem and the temple, and then the signs of his coming (Matthew 24:1–31).

Jesus' first answer covered things that would happen within the next forty years, so let's look at history. Here's what Jesus prophesied and here's what happened.

TIME OF GREAT TROUBLE

Jesus described coming events like earthquakes, famines, false prophets, and a time of "great distress" (Matthew 24:21). In the King James Version of the Bible, "great distress" is called "great tribulation." Some Christians today believe this has not been fulfilled yet. Luke 21:5–32 describes the *exact same signs* as Matthew 24, but there is no talk here about a coming Great Tribulation. Instead Luke describes Jerusalem being destroyed in A.D. 70. So some Christians believe that Jesus was talking *only* about A.D. 70. Others believe he was talking about *both* times of "great distress"—the time of the destruction of the temple and the end of the world.

ARMIES AROUND JERUSALEM

In A.D. 66 the Jews rebelled against Roman rule. Rome struck back that same year, and a Roman commander named Cestius Gallus had his armies surround Jerusalem. Many Christians were trapped in the city. Jesus had warned, "When you see Jerusalem being surrounded by armies, you will know that its desolation is

near. Then let those who are in Judea flee to the mountains, let those in the city get out" (Luke 21:20-21). (Get out? Uh, *yeah*, but *how?*) Suddenly, for no apparent reason, Gallus called off the siege and marched back to the coast. The Jewish zealots raced out of the city to chase him, and the Christians split for a city called Pella. The Romans came back later and

demolished Jerusalem, so it's a good thing the Christians got out. They left because they remembered Jesus' prophecy.

THE FINAL SIEGE

Jesus prophesied, "The days will come upon you when your enemies will build an embankment against you and encircle you and hem you in on every side" (Luke 19:43). In A.D. 70,

the Roman armies were back. This time they
didn't leave. General Titus *did* build walls and
embankments around Jerusalem to hem it in.
His army besieged Jerusalem until people inside
were starving. Then he broke through its walls
and slaughtered its inhabitants.

JERUSALEM LEFT DESOLATE

Jesus said, "There will be great distress in the
land and wrath against this people. They will
fall by the sword and will be taken as prisoners
to all the nations. Jerusalem will be trampled on
by the Gentiles" (Luke 21:23–24). Sad to say,
this is exactly what happened. Some 1,337,490
Jews *were* killed by the Romans. Over 97,000
who survived were taken prisoner and sold as
slaves all over the Roman Empire.

Why did this happen? Jesus said, "I am send-
ing you prophets and wise men and teachers.
Some of them you will kill and crucify; others
you will flog in your synagogues and pursue
from town to town. And so upon you will come
all the righteous blood that has been shed on
earth... all this will come upon this generation...
Look, your house is left to you desolate. For
this is the time of punishment in fulfillment of
all that has been written" (Matthew 23:34–38;
Luke 21:22; see also Luke 23:28). So the
people of Jerusalem were punished by God.

NOT ONE STONE LEFT

Jesus prophesied about the magnificent temple that Herod built for the Jews, "I tell you the truth, not one stone here will be left on another; every one will be thrown down" (Matthew 24:1–2). Well, when the Romans took Jerusalem, many Jewish fighters fled into the temple. Then a Roman soldier threw a torch through a window and set it on fire. The fire was so hot that the gold covering the inside of the temple melted and ran between the cracks of the stones. The Romans later took apart the temple to get the gold. When they were done, not one stone was left upon another. And there was no gold left either.

AFTER THE DESTRUCTION

When Jewish Christians saw Jesus' prophecies being fulfilled, they thought that for sure Jesus would soon return in the clouds. They waited. Years passed. After a while, some Christians decided that Jesus' promise to "come on the clouds" was symbolic. They said that he *had* come when Jerusalem was judged. (After all, Isaiah 19:1 talks about God riding on a cloud when he judged Egypt.)

Other Christians said, "Nuh-uh. We're still waiting for Jesus' return. What happened then was only a *partial* fulfillment of prophecy."

Remember, Jesus' disciples had asked him three separate questions—only one was about the destruction of the temple. The other two were about his return and the end of the age. *Then* Jesus would return and *all* the rest of the prophecies would be fulfilled.

Jesus personally fulfilled many prophecies, but he also made prophecies. And that's another reason to study prophecy. When Jesus was here on earth he talked about Jerusalem being surrounded, the temple being torn down, and so on. The disciples didn't totally understand, but when they saw these things happen, they understood what they needed to do—get out of Jerusalem! Hide out in the mountains! So they did. Hundreds and perhaps thousands of Christians survived physically because they followed Jesus' instructions and kept clear of danger. One of the reasons God gives us prophecy is so we'll know how to respond when we see events taking place. God is looking out for us, but we need to pay attention and do our part.

GET STRONGER

THE AMAZING BOOK OF REVELATION

In A.D. *81, Domitian* became the new emperor of Rome. Now, Dom was okay until he got royally beat up by some wild tribes called Dacians and Marcomanni. That dented Dom's ego so much he made a new law that he be worshiped as *lord and god*. ("You gotta be kidding! You get whipped by the Dacians and you want us to believe you're *God?*") When Christians refused to worship him, Dom began persecuting them.

The Romans grabbed the apostle John, a leader of the church, and shipped him off to the prison island of Patmos. The end? Nope. While John was there, Jesus appeared to him and gave

him a spectacular vision called "the Revelation" (Revelation 1:9). Next year, in A.D. 96, the Romans dumped dumb Dom and got a smarter emperor called Nerva, who had the nerve to allow John to go home.

The book of Revelation was now *big* news! Since it said several times that all the end-time events "must soon take place," and Jesus said, "Behold, I am coming soon!" (Revelation 1:1; 22:12), Christians got excited. They already had the book of Daniel and Matthew 24, so now they began trying to put all the pieces of the puzzle together.

The big theory was that one of the emperors would be the Antichrist (the Beast—Revelation 13) and that Babylon the Great (Revelation 17–18) was the Roman Empire. They believed that the Beast would demand to be worshiped as God and would force everyone to receive his mark (666) in their right hand or forehead. Christians would be killed for refusing. Then Babylon the Great would be destroyed by fire, and Jesus would return to destroy the forces of evil in the Battle of Armageddon. Afterwards Christians would rule earth with Jesus for 1,000 years

(Revelation 20:4).

In the next two centuries after John, Roman emperors like Trajan, Hadrian, Antonius Pius, Marcus Aurelius, Septimius

Severus, Maximin, Decius, Valerian, and Diocletian also demanded to be worshiped as God. They persecuted Christians fiercely. Some of them tortured and killed every Christian they could find. They seemed like the Beast for sure, and lots of early Christians thought that they were.

John wrote, "If anyone has insight, let him calculate the number of the beast, for it is man's number. His number is 666" (Revelation 13:18). Back then, every letter of the Latin alphabet was also a number, so Christians added up the letters of some of these Roman emperor's names to see if they added up to 666. Scary stuff! Sometimes they *did!*

Despite all these terrible persecutions, the end of the world did not come. But Revelation had a great effect: Christians were very comforted by reading it. They knew that one day their suffering would end, and Jesus would return and set up his kingdom on earth.

Stephen was the first martyr mentioned in the Bible—the first Christian who died for his faith. Before he died, Stephen saw Jesus at God's right hand, waiting for him (Acts 7:54–59). Jesus was standing there to take Stephen home before the first rock was thrown. Wow! The next thing Stephen knew was that he was in eternity with Christ. He had a wonderful heavenly home forever and an eternity full of great rewards.

Sometimes we don't want to think about the end-time or the possibility of being persecuted for our faith, but we need to remember that Jesus will be there to lead us to God's throne and comfort us. The Bible says that he will wipe every tear from our eyes and that there

will be no more death, mourning, crying, or pain (Revelation 7:14–17).

Although Bible prophecy is exciting and gives us hope, thinking *too* much about the end-time can sometimes make people focus on God's judgment of the wicked at the end of time. God *does* judge sin and wickedness, but God is love, and his focus in the world right *now* is to love and teach his children and to love others who are not his children and help bring them into God's kingdom. The Bible says, "The Lord is not slow in keeping his promise... He is patient with you, not wanting anyone to perish, but everyone to come to repentance" (2 Peter 3:9). Right now is the time to focus not on God's judgment but on his love and forgiveness.

GET COOLER

Understanding Cool Prophecy Words

There are four major theories about the end-time—Idealist, Preterist, Historicist, and Futurist—and each of these theories has different interpretations of the prophecy words below. In the Preterist viewpoint, it's not exactly *urgent* to understand these terms because, after all, they believe the "end-time" prophecies were fulfilled nearly 2,000 years ago. (It would be like studying history.) Also, the Historicists believe that most prophecies in Revelation were fulfilled *hundreds* of years ago. And Futurists? They're not too concerned about details anyway. They believe it's more important to focus on the *big* picture—that good will conquer evil in the end.

Futurists, however, believe that the events of the end-time are still going to happen—and may happen *soon*. For them, it is *very* important to have a detailed understanding of who the Antichrist might be, what the Mark of the Beast is, etc. That way, if the end-time prophecies are fulfilled in their lifetime, they'll recognize the signs and know what to do. This is why we have mostly given Futurist interpretations to the prophecy words below.

A seven-headed dragon, gigantic demonic locusts, the Rapture, the millennium, the Beast—what *are* all these things? Ever since the book of Revelation came out, end-time prophecy has had a mysterious language of its own. Following are the major cool terms used in Bible prophecy. Knowing them will help you to speak end-time language and give you the tools to crack its incredible code.

THE RAPTURE

The Rapture is when Jesus returns and Christians, dead and alive, rise up to meet him in the air. "Rapture" comes from the Latin word *rapio*, which means "caught up." This comes from 1-Thessalonians 4:17, which says that we "will be caught up... in the clouds to meet the Lord in the air." There are several different opinions as to when the Rapture will take place. The two main theories are called *Pre*-Tribulation Rapture and *Post*-Tribulation Rapture.

PRE-TRIBULATION RAPTURE

Some Christians believe that the first sign that the end has come is that all Christians are secretly, invisibly taken away [raptured] from earth to be with Jesus. According to this theory, shortly after the Christians vanish, the last seven years of world history will begin. Jesus' ultimate return to rule the earth will happen at the end of the seven years. At that time every eyeball will see him.

THE LAST SEVEN YEARS

Daniel 9:27 says, "He will confirm a covenant with many for one 'seven.'" That means for seven years. Daniel prophesied a total of 70 "sevens," and in the Futurist view, the first 69 "sevens" have already been fulfilled, but the last seven years have not happened yet. Many Christians believe that the last seven years will begin soon.

THE ANTICHRIST

John said, "this is the last hour; and as you have heard ... the antichrist is coming..." (1 John 2:18). ("Antichrist" means someone who is "against Christ" or who tries to "take the place of Christ.") Some people believe that "the spirit of the antichrist" (1 John 4:3) has been in many villains down through history, but that there will be one *final* antichrist who will rule the world in the last days. He will persecute the church and lead an army against Christ in the Battle of Armageddon.

THE COVENANT

Daniel 9:27 says, "He will confirm a covenant with many for one 'seven.'" Futurists believe this means that the Antichrist will make a deal (a seven-year covenant) with all the nations of the world. They believe that this will bring world peace, particularly peace in the Middle East. This will allow the Jews to rebuild their temple. Then, in the middle of the seven years, the Antichrist will break the covenant and a time of great trouble will begin.

THE REBUILT JEWISH TEMPLE

Second Thessalonians 2:4 says the Antichrist "sets himself up in God's temple." There are Christians who believe the temple would have to be rebuilt before the Antichrist could take possession. They theorize that the Mosque of Omar which now sits right over the temple site, will either be destroyed or that the temple will be built right beside it.

SEVEN-HEADED DRAGON

Revelation 12:3 describes "an enormous red dragon with seven heads and ten horns and seven crowns on his heads." Verse 9 says this dragon is Satan. Revelation 13:1–2 talks about a *beast* that "had ten horns and seven heads, with ten crowns on his horns"—just like the dragon! Then it says, "The dragon gave the beast his power" to rule over the whole earth (Revelation 13:2,7). So it sounds like the beast is an earthly ruler who copycats his father Satan. Some believe that the Beast is the same guy as the Antichrist (Revelation 13:5).

THE GREAT TRIBULATION

Matthew 24:21 says, "then there will be great distress." (The term "Great Tribulation" comes from the King James Version which says, "then shall be great tribulation.") Some Christians believe this will be the worst time of suffering the earth has ever known. Millions of people will be killed for not following the Antichrist. Some Christians think the entire last seven years are the Great Tribulation; others think the Tribulation is only the last half of the seven years—in other words, the last three and a half years.

THE TEN KINGS

Daniel described a beast in a vision that had ten horns. He also described a great kingdom made up of ten toes (Daniel 2:33,41–44; 7:7–8;). John also described a beast that had ten horns (Revelation 13:1). A popular interpretation is that these ten horns are ten nations existing in the last days that will become part of the Antichrist's kingdom (see Revelation 17:12). Since Europe was once part of the Roman Empire and the ten horns/toes *do* come out of the Roman beast, some Christians believe the ten nations are part of the EEU (European Economic Union). Good guess, but, remember, we don't know for sure.

THE FALSE PROPHET

After talking about the Beast (the Antichrist) in Revelation 13:1–10, John talked about another beast in verses 11–16. This second beast performs miraculous signs and forces the whole world to worship the first Beast and his image. Revelation 19:20 names this second beast "the false prophet." This is why some people think he will be a phony religious leader who supports the Antichrist.

THE MARK OF THE BEAST

Revelation 13:16–18 says that the false prophet will try to force everyone to receive a mark on the right hand or forehead. Anyone who refuses it will not be allowed to buy or sell and will be killed. (And you think shopping is bad *now!*) Since the Bible says that the number of the Beast's name adds up to 666, many Christians think people will have "666" stamped on their forehead. Not very cosmetic! Others guess that the "mark" will be on a tiny computer chip implanted under people's skin and that 666 will be part of everyone's personal ID number. Remember, once again, no one knows for sure what will happen.

THE IMAGE OF THE BEAST

Revelation 13:14–15 talks about the false prophet setting up an image of the Beast for men to worship. The early Christians figured

this was like the statues of the Caesars that Roman citizens worshiped. But since the Bible says that this image can talk (and marble statues can't), some Christians today think this "image" will be a talking robot or supercomputer. The Bible doesn't tell us what it is.

THE ABOMINATION THAT CAUSES DESOLATION

"Abomination" means something awful, and "desolation" is when something is completely destroyed. So when Daniel 9:27 talks about someone setting up "an abomination that causes desolation" in the temple of God, it probably means that something awful trashes the temple. Jesus said that when the abomination that causes desolation is standing in the holy place (the temple) the Great Tribulation would begin (Matthew 24:15, 21). Some Christians think this abomination is the same as the image of the Beast.

TRIBULATION SAINTS

Revelation often talks about "saints" being persecuted by the Beast. Those who believe that Christians vanish out of the world before the last seven years begin think these saints are Jewish people who become believers after Christians are gone. Others believe the tribulation saints are new Christians (Jewish and Gentile) who are saved after the Rapture. Christians who believe that the Rapture doesn't take place 'til the end of the last seven years believe that these saints are Christians who are alive before *and* during the Tribulation. And once again, no one knows for sure.

THE 144,000

Revelation 7 talks about 144,000 people who are sealed by God before the start of the Tribulation. Some people think these 144,000 are Jewish people who will become Christians at this time. Revelation 7:4–14 talks about the 144,000, then talks about a "great multitude ... who have come out of the great tribulation..." So it's possible the 144,000 are special witnesses, or maybe the leaders of the great multitude.

TWO END-TIME WITNESSES

Revelation 11 talks about two witnesses who stand up in Jerusalem to oppose the Beast's reign of terror. They have power like Moses and Elijah to bring down plagues on the earth and breathe out fire to destroy their enemies. There are Christians who think they will be two men such as Moses and Elijah. Others believe they represent two organizations or maybe symbolize the church and the Bible.

THE FOUR HORSEMEN

Revelation 6:1–8 talks about four hideous horsemen. They ride horses that are white, red, black, and pale. The white horse is believed to be either conquest or the Antichrist; the red horse war; the black horse famine; the pale horse death. Some Christians think that these horsemen symbolize the evil that's been in the world since the beginning of time. Others think the horsemen are *worse* wars, famines, and so forth that are released at the start of the Tribulation.

THE TRUMPET PLAGUES

Revelation 8:6–9:21; 11:15–19 describes angels blowing seven

trumpets that start seven plagues on the earth. These plagues are:

- 👁 hail and fire that burn up a third of the earth.

- 👁 a huge burning mountain that falls into the sea.

- 👁 a great burning star that pollutes a third of the rivers.

- 👁 darkness that covers a third of the moon, sun, and stars.

- 👁 a star that releases a demonic locust plague upon the earth.

- 👁 four demons who let 200 million horsemen cross the Euphrates.

- 👁 God takes over the world. Many people also believe this seventh trumpet is the trumpet that signals Jesus' visible, second coming (Matthew 24:31).

There are *so* many interpretations for what these first four plagues are that we couldn't possibly list them all. But let's look at the fifth and sixth plagues.

THE DEMONIC LOCUSTS

Revelation 9:1–11 talks about a mighty swarm of demonic locusts that look like battle horses—only with wings, human faces, long hair, lion's teeth, and iron breastplates. These loco-locusts torment unsaved people on the earth for five months. Some Christians think they're symbols of an invading army. Others think they are actual demons. Some people think John was trying to describe helicopter gun ships.

ARMY OF KILLER HORSES

Revelation 9:13–19 talks about four angels imprisoned in the Euphrates River who lead 200 million savage horses and riders. The horses breathe out fire, smoke, and sulfur, killing one third of the people on earth. It's possible that these horsemen are the "kings from the East" (Revelation 16:12–14) who cross the dried up Euphrates on their way to the Battle of Armageddon (see *Armageddon*). Or they could be something else.

Babylon the Great

Revelation 17 and 18 describe a great prostitute (immoral woman) sitting on the waters. She has a name written on her forehead that reads, "*Mystery Babylon the Great*" (verse 5). This woman is not the ancient kingdom of Babylon. Revelation 17:18 says, "The woman you saw is the great city that rules over the kings of the earth," so some people think Babylon symbolizes Rome or some modern city or nation. In the end, the Beast and ten kings destroy Babylon with fire.

Post-Tribulation Rapture

Post-Tribulation means "after the Tribulation." There are Christians who believe that the

church will go through the Great Tribulation. They believe the Rapture takes place when Jesus returns in the clouds at the end of the seven years. They believe Jesus will rapture his children in front of the entire wicked world when he returns in a blaze of glory—not secretly (Revelation 1:7). First Thessalonians 5:9 says, "For God did not appoint us to suffer wrath," so after the church is raptured, then God begins to pour out his wrath on the wicked who remain (see *Bowls of Wrath*).

THE BOWLS OF WRATH

Many of the trumpet plagues were partial judgments, but when God pours out the seven bowls of the wine of his wrath, there is complete destruction (Revelation 16). Here are the bowls of wrath:

👁 ugly, painful sores on people who have the 666 mark.

👁 the entire sea turns to blood, killing every living thing.

👁 all the rivers and springs of water turn to blood.

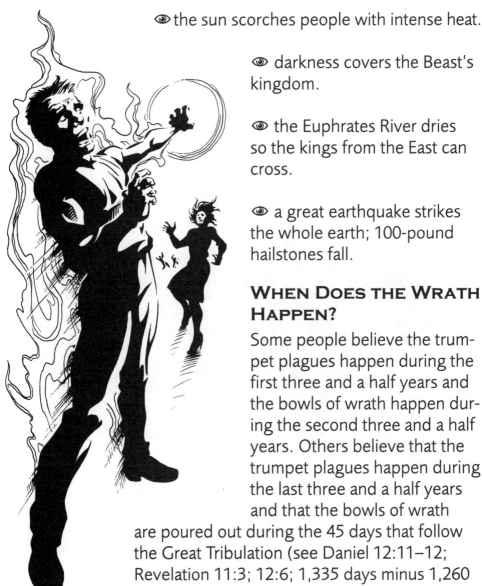

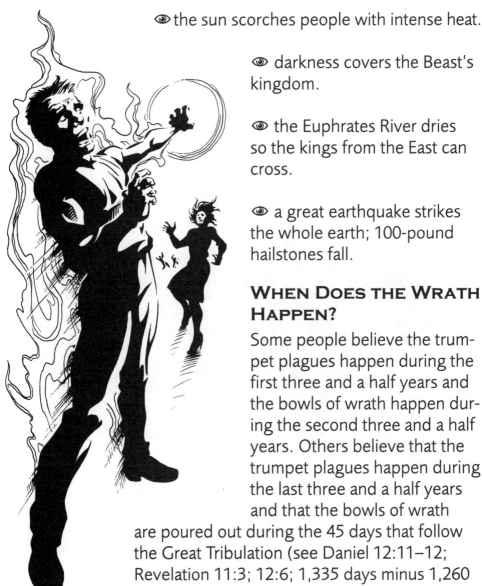the sun scorches people with intense heat.

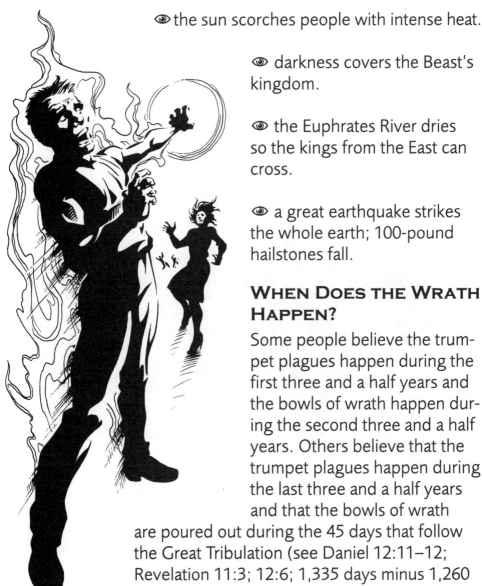 darkness covers the Beast's kingdom.

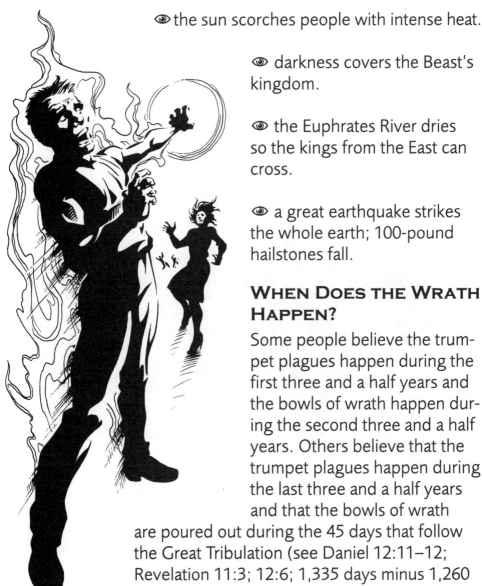 the Euphrates River dries so the kings from the East can cross.

 a great earthquake strikes the whole earth; 100-pound hailstones fall.

WHEN DOES THE WRATH HAPPEN?

Some people believe the trumpet plagues happen during the first three and a half years and the bowls of wrath happen during the second three and a half years. Others believe that the trumpet plagues happen during the last three and a half years and that the bowls of wrath are poured out during the 45 days that follow the Great Tribulation (see Daniel 12:11–12; Revelation 11:3; 12:6; 1,335 days minus 1,260 days = 45 days).

THE BATTLE OF ARMAGEDDON

Revelation 16:14,16 says evil spirits will "go out to the kings of the whole world, to gather them for the battle on the great day of God Almighty" to a place called Armageddon. Armageddon comes from the Hebrew word *har-ma giddôn*, which means "mound of Megiddo." Some believe a great battle will take place around this ancient city mound in the Kishon Valley of Israel. According to this view, the battle will happen when Jesus comes down with the armies of heaven to defeat the armies of the Antichrist (Revelation 19:11–21). It won't be much of a battle, since even *one* angel can defeat an army of 185,000 men (2-Kings 19:35)!

THE JUDGMENT SEAT OF CHRIST

Second Corinthians 5:10 says, "we must all appear before the judgment seat of Christ, that each one may receive what is due him for the things done while in the body, whether good or bad." This is when God rewards Christians for their works (1-Corinthians 3:11–15; Revelation 22:12). The judgment seat of Christ likely happens shortly after the Rapture. The word used for "judgment seat" is the Greek word *bema*. The *bema* was a judge's bench during athletic games where only rewards (*no* punishments) were passed out. You'll go to heaven because Jesus died to save you, but if you want to receive rewards at the *bema*, live your life for God.

THE MILLENNIUM

Revelation 20:4–6 talks about a period of 1,000 years. This is called the Millennium, since that's how you say "thousand years" in Latin. There are three different views on how this prophecy about the Millennium is fulfilled:

Pre-millennialism is the belief that after Jesus returns, there will be a literal Millennium lasting 1,000 years. Jesus will rule over the world as its leader and Christians will reign with him. During this time the earth will be restored to paradise like the Garden of Eden (Isaiah 2:2–5; 11:4–9).

Post-millennialism is the belief that Christians will preach the gospel through the world, conquering more and more, and that Jesus will return after the end of this "millennium" time period to bring about heaven and eternity.

A-millennialism is the belief that Jesus' thousand-year reign is not literal, but symbolic. It symbolizes the ultimate triumph of good over evil.

BATTLE OF GOG AND MAGOG

The Bible says that at the end of the millennium (the thousand-year reign of Christ on earth), the nations will rebel against Christ's rule and be destroyed by fire (Revelation 20:7–10). Some Christians believe that Ezekiel 37–38, which talks about Gog and Magog attacking Israel, is also talking about this battle. Others believe that Ezekiel was talking about the Battle of Armageddon.

GREAT WHITE THRONE JUDGMENT

The Bible says that at the end of the thousand-year millennium the unsaved are raised back to

life, judged, and punished (Revelation 20:11–15). Remember, Christians were raised to life at the beginning of the Millennium, a thousand years earlier.

NEW HEAVEN AND NEW EARTH

After the Great White Throne Judgment, God will make "a new heaven and a new earth" (Revelation 21:1). Possibly this means that God will burn up the earth (2-Peter 3:10), then reform it into a beautiful world with a clean new heaven (atmosphere).

NEW JERUSALEM

Futurists believe that the New Jerusalem is the beautiful city of God that will come down out of heaven and land on earth. Then God will live on earth. Taking the Bible literally, many people believe that the New Jerusalem is about 1,377 miles high, wide, and long—kind of like a big golden cube. Some people believe it will really have streets of gold and an actual river of life. Others like Idealists believe all these descriptions are symbolic and are meant to show that heaven will be unimaginably wonderful (Revelation 21–22).

You'll notice that we often say, "Some people believe" or "the Bible doesn't say for sure." You need to be cautious when you read about prophecy or hear someone say, "The mark of the Beast is definitely a computer code!" Don't automatically believe it. It's *not* like hearing a sermon on salvation or God's love where we can be sure of the simple facts. When people interpret prophecy, they're trying their best to make sense out of mysterious visions and symbols. If the Bible gives the interpretation, *then* we can say we know what it means. If it doesn't, well, listen to someone's interpretation, consider what he or she says but don't think, "Well, it must be true." Also, when you tell others about prophecy, be sure to say, "This is what I *think* it means," or "This is what it could mean."

THINKING OTHERWISE

The first Christians often disagreed over Bible prophecy. They disagreed about how to interpret the book of Daniel, the book of Revelation, and Matthew 24. And that was okay. Everybody agreed on Jesus and salvation, so when it came to Bible prophecy they agreed to disagree.

Famous Christians like Justin Martyr (A.D. 110–165) believed that after Jesus returned he would rule on earth for 1,000 years in the millennium. But Justin knew other Christians didn't believe this. So what did he do? Egg their houses? No. Justin was tolerant of other opinions. He said, "Many who belong to the pure and pious faith, and are true Christians, think otherwise."

Lots of Christians "thought otherwise." Two spiritual leaders, Clement (A.D. 150–215) and Irenaeus (A.D. 130–200) lived at the same time. They agreed on the basics of the faith, but wow, did they *ever* disagree on end-time Bible prophecy!

Irenaeus believed in a literal millennium where Christians would sit around eating giant grapes. *Burrrrp!* Clement thought otherwise. He believed a lot of Bible prophecies were symbolic. He did *not* believe a literal millennium was coming. What about the Antichrist and the Great Tribulation? Clement believed the last days had already happened, that Matthew 24 had all been fulfilled when the Romans destroyed the temple. Like, way back in A.D. 70. All prophecy was done. Finito. No more.

These two guys were cool about their differences. Irenaeus never called Clement a heretic, and Clement never said Irenaeus was a lowlife. But a hundred years later some Christians *were* taking pot shots at each other. Eusebius wrote: "Papias ... says that after the resurrection of the dead there will be a period of a thousand years, when Christ's kingdom will be set up on this earth in material form. I suppose he got these notions by misunderstanding the apos-

tolic accounts and failing to grasp what they had said... For he seems to have been a man of very small intelligence" (*History of the Church* 3:39).

Whoa! *Way to go*, Eusebius! *Not.*

Actually, Eusebius was cool most of the time. He was very smart and loved God. But he had one *eensy* problem: he couldn't understand how anyone could *possibly* have a different interpretation of end-time prophecy from his. If they didn't agree with him, well, they just had to be ... *dumb.*

Better to have Justin Martyr's attitude, huh?

2000 YEARS OF PROPHECY INTERPRETATIONS

For 2,000 years Christians have thought that Bible prophecy was being fulfilled by current events in their day. Here are some ways they interpreted Bible prophecy.

👁 In the years after Jesus, most Christians believed that the Deceiver (Antichrist) would appear and take over the world. Then there would be a time of great trouble. Afterwards would be the sign of Jesus' appearance in heaven, the sound of the trumpet, and the resurrection of the dead (see *Post-Tribulation Rapture*).

👁 A leading Christian named Irenaeus (A.D. 130–200) believed the Roman Empire would break up into ten kingdoms. Then the Antichrist would arrive (Daniel 7:7–8) and rule the world for three and a half years during the Great Tribulation. Then Jesus would return in the clouds, defeat the Antichrist, and set up his millennial kingdom.

👁 Augustine (A.D. 354–430) didn't believe the millennium was a thousand-year period to come. Christianity was the official religion of the Roman Empire, and it was peaceful and cool to be a Christian, so Augustine thought the millennium was already happening.

👁 Six hundred years later, people believed the end-time was still to happen. When the Crusaders began fighting the Muslims in A.D. 1095, they thought that Islam was the Antichrist.

👁 In the Middle Ages, people didn't predict the day that Jesus would return. They believed that the Antichrist would rise first, so they predicted the date of his rise instead.

 In Columbus' day people believed that before Jesus could return, the gospel had to be preached in the entire world. And Jerusalem had to be conquered from the Muslims. So Columbus sailed across the ocean in 1492 to evangelize Asia and find gold to pay for the armies.

 Martin Luther, the famous reformer (1483–1546), thought Pope Leo X was the Antichrist. Nearly all the other Protestant leaders also thought the pope of their day was the Antichrist. They also believed that Christ would return soon.

 By the late 1700s Americans thought the Church of England or the English king was the Antichrist.

THE SUDDEN, SECRET RAPTURE

From Jesus' day 'til about the 1800s, Christians had pretty simple beliefs about end-time events:

👁 the Antichrist would rise,

👁 Christians would be persecuted during the Great Tribulation, then

👁 Jesus would return after the Tribulation, visible to everyone, rapture Christians, and

👁 judge the world.

Then someone came up with the idea of a secret, invisible rapture *before* the Tribulation. No one knows who first came up with this, but John Darby (1800–1882) was the first to really teach it.

Titus 2:12–13 says, "Live self-controlled, upright and godly lives in this present age, while we wait for the blessed hope—the glorious appearing of our great God and Savior, Jesus Christ." Darby said that meant the *very next* prophetic event to happen was *not* the rise of the Antichrist but the return of Jesus!

But a *secret* rapture? Doesn't Revelation 1:7 say, "Look, he is coming with the clouds, and every eye will see him"? True. But Revelation 16:15 says, "Behold, I come like a thief!" Darby believed that Jesus would first come secretly like a thief to rapture the church in the "glorious appearing"—well, *invisible, secret* glorious appearing. Then after the Tribulation he would come back to fight the Battle of Armageddon. *Then* the whole world would see him.

A TWO-THOUSAND-YEAR "INTERRUPTION"

Darby also taught a doctrine called "The Great Parenthesis." No. That is *not* the Great Parent-he-is. A parenthesis are those curvy lines around words (*like this, in fact*) that interrupt a sentence. Darby taught that Daniel's seventy "sevens" prophecy (Daniel 9:24–27) was the history of the Jewish people. After 69 "sevens," when Jesus was crucified, God "interrupted" Jewish history, and the last seven years were postponed.

For 2,000 years of Great Parenthesis, God concentrated on the church. When he was finished with Christians, he would rapture them. Then he would turn his attention back to the Jews

(Romans 11:25–26), and the final seven years of their history would begin. (Whether he was right or wrong you gotta admit, Darby did a lot of thinking about it.)

MILLER'S MIXED-UP MATH

Things were relatively quiet on the prophecy front until the early 1800s. Then things got wild. William Miller was a farmer from Hampton, New York, who got a hundred thousand people very excited about Jesus' return. Miller did his math and decided that Jesus would return between March 21, 1843, and March 21, 1844. After all, the Russians were marching into Turkey at the time. This *had* to be it.

But it wasn't.

Miller and his friends then set a new date: October 22, 1844. ("This is *really it* this time, folks!") Many people quit their jobs, sold their land, closed their businesses, and left their milk cows mooing in the meadows. But when October 22 came and went, folks *really* got bummed out. Well, most of them anyway. Some of Miller's followers continued to set dates for Jesus' return: How about next year— 1845? No? Okay, try 1846. No? Try 1849. Okay, okay, try 1851. Finally most of them got tired of setting dates and went on home to milk their cows.

Some of Miller's followers said that Jesus actually *had* returned October 22, 1844. Only he didn't make it all the way back to earth. Instead he stopped at some heavenly sanctuary out there in space and started going over the books and cleaning out the sanctuary. *Uh-huh*.

Two of Miller's followers named Russell and Barbour started a movement called the Jehovah's Witnesses. They said that Jesus would return to earth and the millennium would begin in 1874. But no one saw Jesus return, and no one was raptured. Then these guys said that, well, he *had* returned and started gathering the saints—only he was, like, invisible.

Russell believed the saints would all be gathered by 1881.

When Jesus still didn't come, Russell set new dates: Jesus would return, *absolutely for sure—this is it this time, folks*—in 1914! He didn't, so Russell threw in another four years: 1918 was the date. Jesus didn't return then either. So the Jehovah's Witnesses began setting more dates for Jesus' return: first 1925, then 1975, and then 1984. While the Jehovah's Witnesses were busy setting dates, something else was happening.

ISRAEL BECOMES A NATION

When Jerusalem was destroyed in A.D. 70, the Jews were scattered all over the Roman world and there was no longer a nation of Israel. At the end of the 1800s the Jews wanted to return to their old land, which was now called Palestine. Many Christians agreed. They said that for end-time prophecy to be fulfilled, the Jews *had* to return and become a nation again. During World War I the British took over Palestine, and in 1917, they allowed the Jews to return and settle there. This got many Christians excited. And they *really* got excited when

Israel declared its independence on May 14, 1948, and became a nation again! "Now," people thought, "the end-time is *finally* here!"

THE FIG TREE

After talking about the Great Tribulation and his return, Jesus said, "Now learn this lesson from the fig tree: As soon as its twigs get tender and its leaves come out, you know that summer is near. Even so, when you see all these things, you know that it is near, right at the door. I tell you the truth, this generation will certainly not pass away until all these things have happened" (Matthew 24:32–34).

In 1970 a Christian author named Hal Lindsey wrote a book called *The Late Great Planet Earth*. In it, he said that the fig tree symbolized the nation of Israel. Its leaves budding was the nation of Israel coming back to life after 2,000 years. He guessed that Jesus would return soon. He wrote that "within forty years or so of 1948 (when Israel became a nation again), all these things could take place."

Since a biblical generation often lasted forty years (and 1948 plus 40 = 1988) this meant, hey, Jesus might return by 1988.

One pastor was even more specific. He said that Jesus was going to rapture the church (secret rapture) before the end of 1981. (This left room for the last seven years to happen before 1988.) Another writer wrote a book titled *88 Reasons Why the Rapture Will Be in 1988*. (Hmmm ... I wonder if that book is still in print?)

When Jesus didn't return in 1981 or 1988, people recalculated and said, "Well, a generation doesn't *have* to be forty years. It could be like, seventy years, or eighty years or hey!— even a hundred years. A generation means the length of a normal person's life. Jesus could *still* come in one very long generation from 1948!"

It all goes back to the theory that Israel is the fig tree. But nowhere does the Bible say, "This fig tree symbolizes Israel." If you want to believe that it's Israel, that's fine. If you want to read Hal Lindsey's book or any other book on end-time Bible prophecy, that's fine too. Just be sure that you know the difference between what the *Bible* says and what are only men's interpretations. You can trust God's Word. You can't trust men's guesses. A guess is not a fact. A guess is a guess.

ENTERING A NEW MILLENNIUM

Many Christians believe that the world was created about 6,000 years ago, and that these six millennia symbolize the first six days of Creation. So the seventh day of creation (day seven, when God rested) would be the thousand-year Millennium (Genesis 2:2; 2-Peter 3:8). As the year 2000 approached, they thought that it was time for the Millennium to happen.

Books predicting 2000 and 2001 as the date of the Millennium's start were published and sold. Bible prophecy preachers on television said that Jesus would return "right around 2000." On top of it, many people believed that a computer error would cause all the world's computers to crash at midnight, the first minute of the new millennium. They didn't crash, and we're all still here.

PREDICTIONS WITHOUT END

Jesus said no one could know the day of his return, but for 2,000 years zealous Christians have been predicting dates for the rise of the Antichrist or the second coming of Jesus.

👁 In A.D. 410, the Visigoths attacked Rome. Roman Christians thought the end of the world had come!

👁 When the Mongols and Turks invaded Europe, Catholics believed these guys were the armies of Gog and Magog (Ezekiel 38).

👁 In 1191 a Bible scholar named Joachim of Fiore told Richard the Lionhearted that the

Antichrist had already been born and was alive some-where in the world.

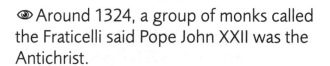 People predicted that the Antichrist would rise in 1184. *No?* Well, how about 1229? *No?* Okay, try 1260. Not *then* either? Okay, okay, take your pick! He'll either rise in 1300, 1325, 1335, 1346, 1387, or 1400. Every one of these dates was believed by thou-sands of Christians.

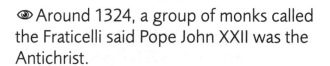 Around 1324, a group of monks called the Fraticelli said Pope John XXII was the Antichrist.

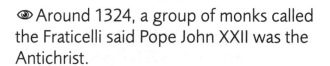 When the Black Plague reached Europe in 1347, people thought it was an end-time plague. They thought that the Antichrist would soon rise.

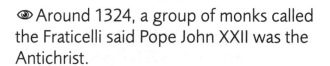 A Christian leader, Jan Hus (1371–1415), said that the pope was the Antichrist.

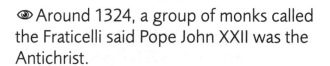 The Taborites predicted that the world would end in February 1420. When that

didn't happen, they sold all their belongings, formed armies, and began killing non-Taborites. *Man,* were they ticked off about being wrong!

👁 In the 1400s a crazy group called the Adamites said that all the prophecies had been fulfilled and the millennium had begun. They thought they were just like Adam and Eve in the Garden of Eden, so they ran around naked. *Okaaaaay.*

👁 Martin Luther, the famous reformer (1483–1546), thought the end of the world would happen about 1600. He later guessed it would happen about 2000.

👁 Thomas Müntzer (1488–1525), a Protestant, ordered his followers to take up arms to fight the Antichrist—whom he thought was the pope.

👁 Melchior Hofmann (1495–1543), another Protestant leader, predicted that Jesus would return in 1533. He also predicted that Strasbourg, Germany, would be New Jerusalem (Revelation 21). His followers later claimed Münster was the New Jerusalem.

👁 When Oliver Cromwell (1599–1658) was leader of England, two of his guards thought that they were the end-time witnesses of Revelation 11.

👁 The monarchists believed that between 1655 and 1657 England would lead Christians to defeat the pope, destroy the Antichrist, and reconquer Jerusalem.

👁 People were terrified as the year 1666 approached. After all, 666 is the number of the Antichrist (Revelation 13:18).

👁 Christians later predicted the world would end in 1689, then in 1694, then in 1697, then 1705, then 1706, then 1708, then 1716, then 1736, and then 1795.

👁 By 1773 many Americans believed the British king, George III, was the Antichrist. They thought that if they won the Revolutionary War, the millennium would begin on earth. Where? Why, in America, of course.

👁 The Mormons thought America was indeed the Promised Land and worked to build New Jerusalem in Utah.

👁 William Miller said that Jesus would return between March 21, 1843, and March 21, 1844. When that didn't happen, he set a new date: October 22, 1844. Later, some of his followers said Jesus would return in 1845. Then 1846. Then 1849. Then 1851.

👁 The Jehovah's Witnesses said Jesus would return in 1874. Then they said 1881, 1914, 1918, 1925, 1975, and finally 1984.

👁 Some of the latest guys that were labeled the Antichrist were the pope, Mussolini, Hitler, Gorbachev, Ronald Reagan, and Saddam Hussein.

Jesus told his disciples, "the Son of Man will come at an hour when you do not expect him" (Matthew 24:44). He added, "No one knows about that day or hour" (Matthew 24:36). He finally flat-out said, "It is not for you to know the times or dates the father has set" (Acts 1:7). You'd think people would get the hint? No, for 2,000 years some people have simply not been able to resist predicting the year of Jesus' return—as if knowing that date was the most important thing they needed to do. So don't be surprised if some people you know do this some day. If it happens, the best thing to do is just smile and take it with a grain of salt. There's nothing wrong with having a good discussion, but don't get into big arguments about Bible prophecy.

FOUR DIFFERENT WAYS TO LOOK AT BIBLE PROPHECY

THE MAJOR THEORIES

Some Bible prophecy books predict dates and insist that current world events are fulfilling Bible prophecy. The end is at hand! This gets people very excited, so these books sell wagonloads of copies. Because so many people read these theories, they become popular belief among Christians. Soon the theory becomes accepted as fact, and many people think this is what "everyone" believes. This isn't the case. There are at least four major ways of looking at

how the events of the end-time will unfold. Each view represents a large number of people who believe that their view is correct and that the others are wrong. Here's a summary of those basic viewpoints. See what you think.

Preterists: First there are preterists (*pree*-ter-ists). They believe that all the last days prophecies in Revelation and Matthew 24 were fulfilled when the Roman general Titus destroyed Jerusalem in A.D. 70 (or 90 at latest). Preterists are not waiting for the Antichrist to rise and brand people with the mark of the Beast. They are not waiting for the Battle of Armageddon. They believe it's already fulfilled.

Preterists believe that Jesus came in the clouds in A.D. 70. Ever since he has been ruling the world through the church, conquering more people all the time. They think the last two thousand years have been like the millennium. While the world may look bad, it's up to Christians to change it. Through the preaching of the gospel, God's righteousness will eventually triumph over the world. When the whole world has been won, then Jesus hands over the kingdom to his Father (1-Corinthians 15:24–25).

If you're convinced that we're living in the last days, you may think preterists must be crazy. But preterists like to point out:

👁 A lot of Jesus' prophecies in Matthew 24 and Luke 21 *were* fulfilled in A.D. 70.

👁 When talking to his disciples in A.D. 30, Jesus said, "this generation will certainly not pass away until all these things have happened" (Matthew 24:34). And Jesus had just finished talking about his second coming.

👁 Jesus *did* say, "the Son of Man is going to come in his Father's glory with his angels, and then he will reward each person according to what he has done. I tell you the truth, some who are standing here will not taste death before they see the Son of Man coming in his kingdom" (Matthew 16:27–28). Preterists believe that since these two sentences are together, they must be talking about the same event.

Historicists: Historicists say that most things in the book of Revelation talk about wars and events in Western Europe during the past 2,000 years.

For example, some believe that the first four trumpet judgments are talking about the fall of the Roman Empire. They believe the first trumpet judgment, "hail and fire mixed with blood" (Revelation 8:6–7) was the Goths invading Italy in 410.

What about the second trumpet, the huge burning mountain that was thrown into the sea? Historicists say it was the Vandals conquering Gaul, Spain, and North Africa in 422 (Revelation 8:8–9). The "great star, blazing like a torch" (Revelation 8:10–11)—was Attila the Hun in 440. The locust plague of the fifth trumpet? Muslim armies conquering from 600 to 700.

Mind you, some historicists believe that *not all* of Revelation has been fulfilled in history already—some of the events are still to be

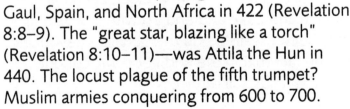

fulfilled. For example, they are still waiting for the visible second coming of Christ and his millennial reign on earth for a thousand years.

Idealists: Idealists believe that the book of Revelation is the Word of God, but they don't think it's talking about literal battles and literal people. They believe it's speaking in symbolic language. It's all a nonspecific battle between good and evil. Idealists would say, "Well, you do have to admit, a lot of the stuff in Revelation *is* symbolic. When was the last time you saw a red dragon with seven heads chasing a woman standing on the moon?" (Revelation 12:1-3.)

Idealists don't think the details in Revelation are to be taken literally and lined up with world events. They believe that Jesus will come back, but they don't believe that you can use Revelation to figure out exactly how and when. Idealists don't spend their time figuring out which world leader is the Antichrist. They don't put together verses from Ezekiel, Zechariah, Daniel, and Luke and end up with a puzzle of prophecy. Idealists skip the details. They focus on the fact that in the end good will conquer evil and Jesus will return.

Futurists: Futurists believe that most of the prophecies in the Bible have not been fulfilled yet. These will happen in the last days, which are still to happen. Futurists believe that most of the prophecies of Daniel and Revelation, Matthew 24, Ezekiel 38–39, parts of 1-Corinthians 15, Isaiah, 1 and 2-Thessalonians, Malachi, Zechariah, and oodles of other verses are still going to happen.

Remember the famous seventy "sevens" (Daniel 9:25–27)? Futurists believe that the first 69 "sevens" have already been fulfilled but that the last seven years are *yet* to be fulfilled. The Tribulation, the Antichrist, the mark of the Beast, and worldwide persecution of Christians are still to happen. And probably soon.

Most futurists believe there will be a literal mark of the Beast. They believe that the wars and plagues of the Great Tribulation will wipe out millions and millions of people. All the armies of the world will actually gather together in the Valley of Armageddon to make war against Jesus and his heavenly army. Then there will be 1,000 years of Jesus' rule on the earth. After that, God will remake the earth and New Jerusalem will come down out of heaven.

There are lots of different kinds of futurists, but the main groups believe either in *Pre*-Tribulation Rapture or in *Post*-Tribulation Rapture.

Pre-Tribulation Rapture—Many Christians believe that the first sign the end has come is that all Christians will be suddenly raptured [taken up] from earth secretly and invisibly. Then, after the Christians have vanished, the last seven years of world history will begin and the Antichrist will take over. Then the trumpet judgments sound and the bowls of wrath are poured out. Jesus then returns at the end of the seven years to fight the Battle of Armageddon. Everyone will see him return at that time.

Post-Tribulation Rapture—Many Christians believe that the church will still be on earth and go through the Great Tribulation. They will witness for Christ and suffer persecution for his name, even being martyred. They will live through the trumpet plagues. They believe the Rapture takes place when Jesus returns in the clouds at the end of the seven years. It will not

be a secret, invisible rapture but Jesus rescu-
ing his children in front of the entire world as
he returns in a blaze of glory (Revelation 1:7).
After that are the bowls of wrath, then Jesus
returns to fight the Battle of Armageddon.

In Conclusion

When the disciples asked Jesus, "Lord, are you at this time going to restore the kingdom to Israel?" he answered, "It is not for you to know the times or dates the Father has set by his own authority. But you will receive power when the Holy Spirit comes on you; and you will be my witnesses ... to the ends of the earth'-" (Acts 1:6–8). Get that? God's job is handling the future and making end-time events happen. Our job is living the truth and sharing it with others.

We don't know when Jesus is returning, and we don't *need* to know. Jesus said, "be ready, because the Son of Man will come at an hour when you do not expect him" (Luke 12:40). Jesus will come at the right time. In the meantime, we need to obey God and be prepared for his coming every day—and to get out the gospel.

And what happens when the whole world has heard? Jesus said, "this gospel of the kingdom will be preached in the whole world ... to all nations, and then the end will come" (Matthew 24:14). When the whole world has had a chance to hear the good news about Jesus and make their choice, then Jesus will return, right all wrong, and bring heaven on earth! What a wonderful day that will be!

We should be excited about Jesus' second coming and the thought of spending eternity with him. That's why it's important to study end-time prophecy. The Bible says that we should read prophecy and take it to heart (Revelation 1:3). But as we do that, let's remember that our job is living for Jesus and sharing our faith with others. God will take care of the future.

In every good story, there's a point where all seems lost, dark, and awful for the heroes. But then there's a dramatic climax where the good guys win and evil is defeated. And this is what happens in the Bible. The book of Revelation describes the dark drama that happens just before God wins the ultimate battle. So remember, Jesus is coming! Good *will* triumph over evil!

Don't focus on the scary things or the things in Bible prophecy that confuse you. Instead, think about the fantastic, happy ending that's coming. Think about how wonderful it will be ruling and reigning on earth with Jesus! You think life has cool things in it now? Ho! Wait 'til you see what the future holds! Everything that is so important to you now will look like cheap imitations once you see the real deal in heaven.

"And so we will be with the Lord forever. Therefore encourage each other with these words" (1-Thessalonians 4:17–18).

What is  2:52 SOUL GEAR ?

Based on Luke 2:52:
"And Jesus grew in wisdom and stature,
and in favor with God and men (NIV)."

2:52 is designed just for boys 8-12!
This verse is one of the only verses in
the Bible that provides a glimpse of Jesus
as a young boy. Who doesn't wonder what
Jesus was like as a kid?

Become smarter, stronger, deeper,
and cooler as you develop
into a young man of God
with 2:52 Soul Gear™!

Zonder**kidz**

The 2:52 Soul Gear™ takes a closer look by focusing on the four major areas of development highlighted in Luke 2:52:

"Wisdom" = mental/emotional = **Smarter**

"Stature" = physical = **Stronger**

vor with God" = spiritual = **Deeper**

Favor with men" = social = **Cooler**

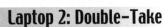

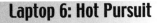

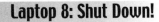

The 2:52 Boys Bible–
the "ultimate manual" for boys!

The 2:52 Boys Bible, NIV
Features written by Rick Osborne

Become more like Jesus mentally, physically, spiritually, and socially–Smarter, Stronger, Deeper, and Cooler—with the 2:52 Boys Bible!

Hardcover 0-310-70320-4
Softcover 0-310-70552-5

from Inspirio...

CD Holder   ISBN: 0-310-99033-5

Book & Bible Holder

Med   ISBN: 0-310-98823-3

Large ISBN: 0-310-98824-1

Coming February 2005...

Another "straight from the pages of the Bible" ACTION & ADVENTURE book!

Big Bad Bible Giants

Written by Ed Strauss

It's all about giants, some in the Bible and some not. Helping you get smarter, stronger, deeper, and cooler, *Big Bad Bible Giants* is full of facts that will fascinate even the most inquisitive reader.

Softcover 0-310-70869-9

Coming February 2005

A new four-book series filled with adventure, mystery, and intrigue as three friends—Dan, Peter, and Shelby, seek to discover the hidden mysteries of Eckert House!

2:52 Mysteries of Eckert House: Hidden in Plain Sight (Book 1)

Written by Chris Auer
Softcover 0-310-70870-2

2:52 Mysteries of Eckert House: A Stranger, a Thief, and a Pack of Lies (Book 2)

Written by Chris Auer
Softcover 0-310-70871-0

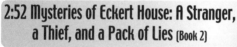

2:52 Mysteries of Eckert House: The Chinese Puzzle Box (Book 3)

Written by Chris Auer
Softcover 0-310-70872-9

2:52 Mysteries of Eckert House: The Forgotten Room (Book 4)

Written by Chris Auer
Softcover 0-310-70873-7

Zonderkidz.

We want to hear from you. Please send your comments
about this book to us in care of the address below.
Thank you.

Zonder**kidz**.

Grand Rapids, MI 49530
www.zonderkidz.com